MARIO TIME!

By Courtney Carbone

Designed by Melanie Bermudez Cerna

Random House 🏠 New York

™ & © 2024 Nintendo. All rights reserved. Published in the United States by Random House Children's Books, a division of Penguin Random House LLC, 1745 Broadway, New York, NY 10019, and in Canada by Penguin Random House Canada Limited, Toronto. Random House and the colophon are registered trademarks of Penguin Random House LLC. Originally published in slightly different form by Random House Books for Young Readers in 2018.

ISBN 978-0-593-80943-3 (trade)
rhcbooks.com
MANUFACTURED IN CHINA
10 9 8 7 6 5 4 3 2

SUPER MARIO BROS.

Mario has been on lots of adventures over the years. In fact, he has been featured in over 200 Nintendo games! While gameplay and graphics have evolved with each new release, Mario's quest to save the day remains the same. Here is a look back at the original Super Mario Bros. franchise.

DID YOU KNOW?
Super Mario Bros. is the bestselling video game series of all time!

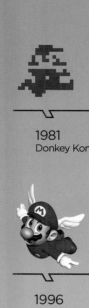

1981
Donkey Kong

1983
Mario Bros.

1985
Super Mario Bros.

1988
Super Mario Bros. 2

1990
Super Mario Bros. 3

1991
Super Mario World

1996
Super Mario 64

2002
Super Mario Sunshine

2006
New Super Mario Bros.

2007
Super Mario Galaxy

2009
New Super Mario Bros. Wii

2010
Super Mario Galaxy 2

2011
Super Mario 3D Land

2012
New Super Mario Bros. 2

2012
New Super Mario Bros. U

2013
Super Mario 3D World

2015
Super Mario Maker

2016
Super Mario Run

MARIO TIME LINE

DID YOU KNOW?
Shigeru Miyamoto is the creator of Super Mario Bros.

2017
Super Mario Odyssey

What is **YOUR** favorite game?

_____

Mario is a heroic plumber who goes on quests to help his friends and save the day. He frequently comes to the rescue of his beloved Princess Peach, who is often kidnapped by the evil villain Bowser in an attempt to gain control over all of Mushroom Kingdom.

WHAT DO YOU THINK MARIO WILL LOOK LIKE NEXT?

Name: Mario
Residence: Unknown
Occupation: Plumber
Signature Style: Red "M" hat, red shirt, blue overalls, and dark, bushy mustache

DID YOU KNOW?
Contrary to popular belief, Mario's first save was not Princess Peach, but another woman, named Pauline.

Background

Mario was first seen in the video game **Donkey Kong**, which came out in 1981. His character was a carpenter known as Jumpman. Later, he was almost called Mr. Video, but instead was named Mario, after the landlord of a Nintendo building in the United States.

3, 2, 1, Draw!

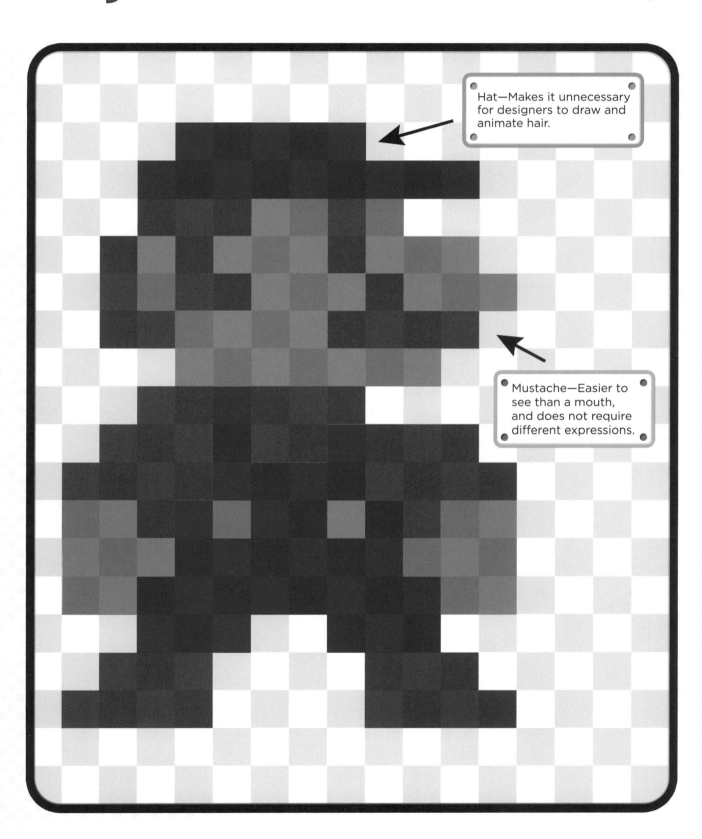

Hat—Makes it unnecessary for designers to draw and animate hair.

Mustache—Easier to see than a mouth, and does not require different expressions.

Mario has become one of the most recognizable characters in the world. But did you know that his look was strategically chosen by his creators? Use the image on the facing page to learn how to draw Mario. Take it box by box.

LUIGI

Luigi is Mario's brother. While this tall hero generally plays Mario's sidekick, he does occasionally take the lead, as in **Luigi's Mansion**.

Name: Luigi
Residence: Unknown
Occupation: Plumber
Signature Style: Green "L" hat, green shirt, blue overalls, and dark, bushy mustache

Background

Luigi was introduced in the arcade game **Mario Bros.** in 1983, to provide gamers with a two-player option. He looked very similar to Mario, but with green clothes instead of red. Soon he was given his own identity, complete with a growth spurt and a personality all his own.

Both Mario and Luigi have look-alike archrivals who often get in the way of their adventures. While Wario and Waluigi may resemble their hero counterparts, make no mistake—they are only looking to cause trouble!

DOUBLE TROUBLE!

Imagine and draw your archrival. To name your character, replace the first letter of your name with "W" or "Wa."

Name: _____

PRINCESS PEACH

Princess Peach rules benevolently over Mushroom Kingdom, bringing peace and prosperity to her loyal subjects, the Toads.

Name: Peach
Residence: Mushroom Kingdom
Occupation: Princess of Mushroom Kingdom
Signature Style: Blond hair, pink dress, gold tiara, and white gloves

Background

Princess Peach first appears in **Super Mario Bros.**, where she is credited in the game manual as Princess Toadstool. In **Super Mario 64**, she writes a letter to Mario, signing it both "Princess Toadstool" and "Peach," acknowledging that the characters are one and the same.

DID YOU KNOW?
Princess Peach has been in more video games than any other female character in history!

PRINCESS DAISY

Princess Daisy is the caring ruler of Sarasaland. When her kingdom was taken over by the evil purple space monster Tatanga, Mario helped her restore order and bring peace back to her land.

Name: Daisy
Residence: Sarasaland
Occupation: Princess of Sarasaland
Signature Style: Brown hair, yellow-and-orange dress, gold tiara, and white gloves

Background

Princess Daisy first appeared in **Super Mario Land** in 1989, the first Mario title produced for the Game Boy handheld console. Since then, she has become a favorite playable character throughout the franchise.

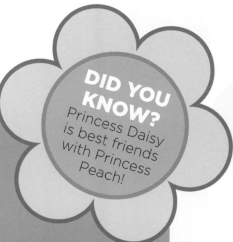

DID YOU KNOW?
Princess Daisy is best friends with Princess Peach!

Sarasaland has four distinct kingdoms. Hold this page up to a mirror to find out their names!

BIRABUTO, MUDA, EASTON, AND CHAI.

BOWSER

Bowser is a bad-tempered fire-breathing villain whose goal is to kidnap Princess Peach and take over Mushroom Kingdom (and beyond). For this reason, he is Mario's archenemy, and frequently battles him and his allies.

Name: Bowser
Residence: Unknown
Occupation: King of the Koopas
Signature Style: Yellow body, red hair, sharp horns, spiky shell, and armbands

Background

Bowser and Mario have been fighting since 1985, when the first **Super Mario Bros.** game was released. Back then, Bowser was the final boss Mario needed to defeat to claim victory and rescue the princess.

WHAT IS BOWSER'S EVIL LAUGH?

A. "Tee-hee-hee!"

B. "Bwa-ha-ha!"

C. "Heh-heh-heh!"

D. "Hardy-har-har!"

See page 64 for all answers.

MINION MIGHT

Bowser has lots of loyal minions to help carry out his evil plans, including the Koopalings and his son, Bowser Jr. Help Mario match the Koopalings with their names by circling them in the puzzle. Answers can be up, down, forward, or backward.

I	E	V	Q	L	E	M	M	Y	T	S	E	V	R
H	U	O	P	A	H	V	O	B	N	T	M	O	J
G	L	Y	E	R	S	E	R	C	T	V	G	Z	R
U	A	E	A	O	B	C	T	M	F	E	I	G	E
U	R	I	P	Y	E	Z	O	E	M	G	W	L	S
V	R	C	E	S	V	E	N	P	Y	L	D	O	W
T	Y	I	O	A	Q	W	D	S	G	R	U	C	O
C	O	W	E	N	D	Y	E	S	G	V	L	H	B
D	E	V	E	I	P	S	U	S	I	N	C	X	E

LARRY   IGGY   WENDY
LEMMY   LUDWIG   ROY
MORTON   BOWSER Jr.

YOSHI

Yoshi is good-natured and often accompanies Mario on his travels. Yoshi has the ability to hatch eggs, eat enemies, and spit objects as an attack. He can also communicate with both humans and other Yoshis!

Name: Yoshi
Residence: Unknown
Occupation: Sidekick
Signature Style: Green body, red shell, and orange boots

Background

Mario and Yoshi meet in **Super Mario World** (1990), when Mario releases Yoshi from an egg hidden in a ? Block. Yoshi introduces himself and says that Bowser trapped him on his way to rescue his friends. Since then, Yoshi has been featured—and has even starred—in many other games, including **Super Mario World 2: Yoshi's Island** (1995); **Yoshi's Story** (1997); and **Yoshi's Woolly World** (2015).

DID YOU KNOW?
Yoshi is an omnivore, which means he eats both plants and animals.

TOAD

Toad is a friendly mushroom-shaped fellow who is the royal attendant to Princess Peach and a sidekick to Mario. He is always up for a good time and loves going on adventures with his friends.

Name: Toad
Residence: Mushroom Kingdom
Occupation: Royal Attendant
Signature Style: Red-and-white head, blue vest, white shorts, and brown shoes

Background

Toad first appears in ***Super Mario Bros. (1985)*** and becomes one of the four playable character options in ***Super Mario Bros. 2 (1988)***, along with Mario, Luigi, and Princess Peach. Each of the character choices includes a unique skill. Toad's special ability is to quickly pick up items with his super strength. Toad soon became a fan favorite, and appeared in more games.

TOADETTE

Toadette is a fun-loving adventurer. While she and Captain Toad are out treasure hunting, she is kidnapped when she tries to keep a Power Star out of the clutches of a giant bird named Wingo.

Name: Toadette
Residence: Mushroom Kingdom
Occupation: Adventurer
Signature Style: Pink-and-white pigtailed head, pink dress, red vest, white shorts, and brown shoes

Background

Toadette is first introduced as Toad's racing partner in *Mario Kart: Double Dash!!* (2003). She is frequently a playable character in racing games and is one of the only Toads to costar in her own game, *Captain Toad: Treasure Tracker* (2014).

SUPER MARIO MEMORY CARDS!

1. Cut out the playing cards.
2. Shuffle the cards and arrange them facedown on a flat surface.
3. Turn the cards over two at a time.
4. If you match two characters, remove them from game play and go again.
5. If you match two Bowsers or two Goombas, you automatically lose the game. Better luck next time!
6. If the cards do not match, turn them back over in the same place.
7. Repeat (or take turns with your friend) until all the characters are matched and only the Bowser and Goomba cards are left.

One player: If you are playing alone, see how few turns it takes to match all the cards!

Two players: If you are playing with a friend, whoever has more matches at the end of the game wins!

Hint: If you turn over a Bowser or Goomba card, turn over a card that you have seen before so you don't risk turning over the matching villain card!

SUPER MARIO SUPER MARIO SUPER MARIO SUPER MARIO SUPER MARIO

SUPER MARIO SUPER MARIO SUPER MARIO SUPER MARIO SUPER MARIO

SUPER MARIO SUPER MARIO SUPER MARIO SUPER MARIO SUPER MARIO

SUPER MARIO SUPER MARIO SUPER MARIO SUPER MARIO SUPER MARIO

SUPER MARIO SUPER MARIO SUPER MARIO SUPER MARIO SUPER MARIO

SUPER MARIO SUPER MARIO SUPER MARIO SUPER MARIO SUPER MARIO

TOAD TROUBLE!

As part of a new plan to take over Mushroom Kingdom, Bowser has sent an imposter Toad to live among the real ones. Can you stop him by spotting the fake in the picture?

MARIO BOXES

With a friend (or foe), take turns connecting two dots with a straight line. If the line you draw completes a box, put your initials in it and take another turn. Count one point for squares containing your initials. If a box you completed contains a Toad, give yourself two points. When all the boxes are completed, the player with more points wins!

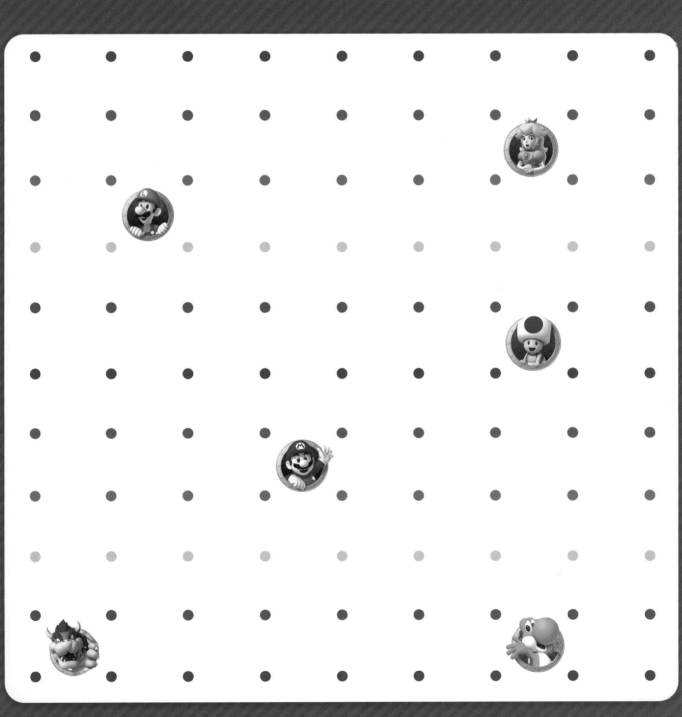

PLAY AGAIN!

Mario knows that it takes patience and strategy to defeat his most stubborn enemies. Play the box game again to see who wins!

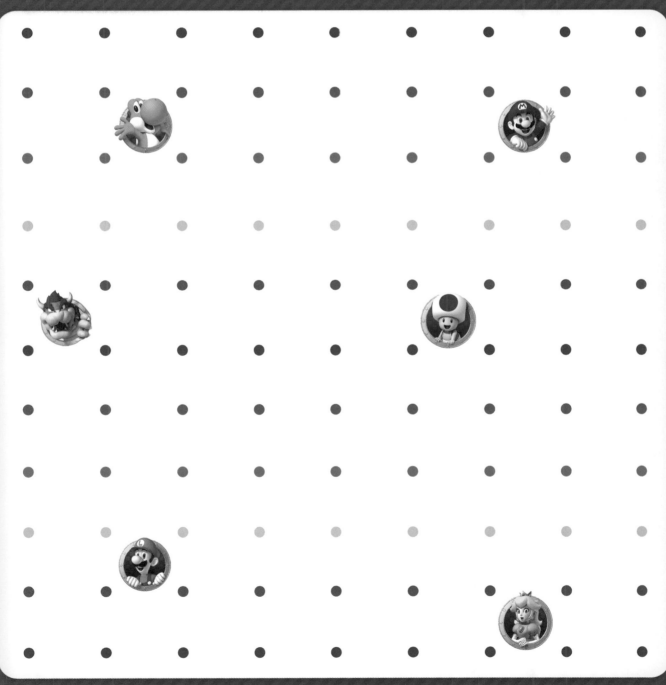

BETTER HALF

The characters in **Super Mario Bros.** have evolved greatly over time, from 8-bit images to fully rendered characters. Now it's your turn to be the artist! Finish drawing each character, using the halves shown below as guides.

CHAIN CHOMP

During his quests, Mario often encounters villains that look like giant balls and chains, known as Chain Chomps. You can make your own Chain Chomp by following the instructions on the back of this page.

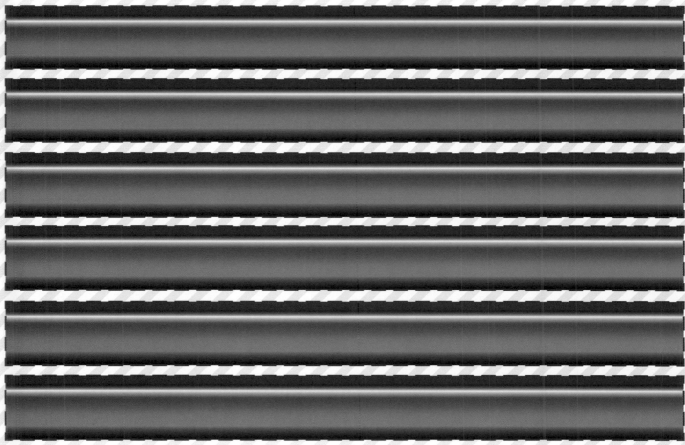

CHAIN CHOMP

Instructions

1. Cut out the strips and face.
2. Create a ring with the first strip.
3. Fasten the ends of the ring with tape.
4. Loop another strip through the first ring.
5. Repeat the process until you have a full chain.
6. Attach the face to the end of the chain with tape.

Create your own ? Block by following the instructions.

1. Carefully cut out the boxes.
2. Fold the paper inward along the edges.
3. Tape the bottom and sides together.
4. Fold the top in place, and use the tab to keep it closed.

When you are finished, follow the same steps on the second block to create a die for the board game on pages 36 and 37.

Hint: Feel free to put a small item in your ? Block.

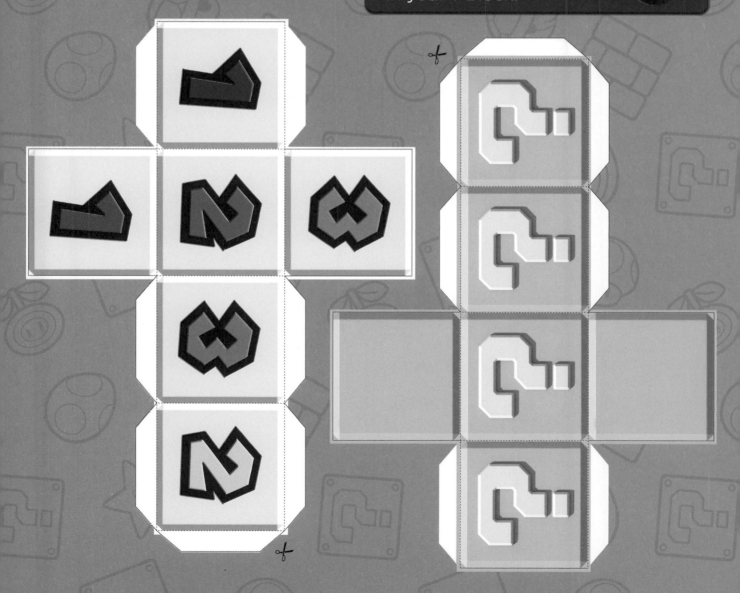

PAPER CRAFT FUN

LOUD AND CLEAR!

Mario has many famous catchphrases.
Use the code to translate some of them.

BOARD GAME

How to Play

1. Use buttons or coins as pieces. Place your pieces on **START** and take turns rolling the die from p. 33 to move.
2. Move forward the number of spaces shown on the die. Then use the key to follow the instructions on that space.
3. The first person to reach **FINISH** is the winner!

START

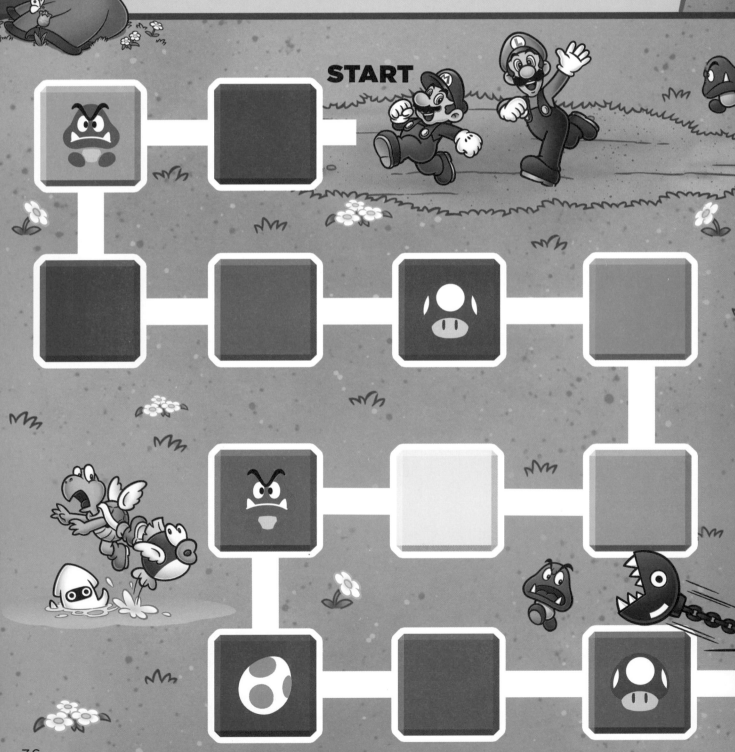

Key

⭐ Go forward 5 spaces.
🍄 Go backward 2 spaces.
🍄 Go forward 2 spaces.
🥚 Go forward 5 spaces.
👹 Go back to START.

FINISH

37

TOAD BOXES

With a friend, take turns connecting two dots with
a straight line. If the line you draw completes a box,
put your initials in it and take another turn. Count
one point for squares containing your
initials. If a box you completed contains
a Toad, give yourself two points.
When all the boxes are completed,
the player with more points wins!

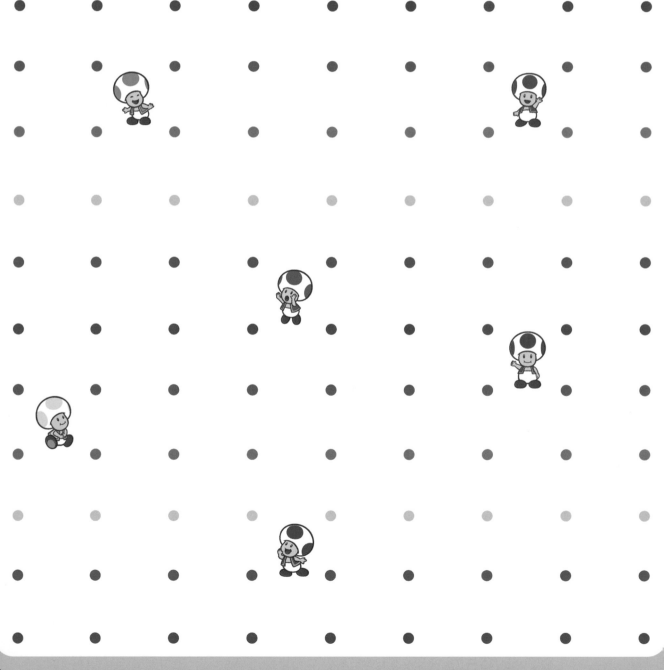

SPOT THE DIFFERENCES!

Mario has many friends and many foes.
Can you find all five differences between these two pictures?

PIPE MAZE

As a plumber, Mario knows his way around underground pipes. Draw a path through the pipes to help him avoid Koopas, Piranha Plants, and Goombas!

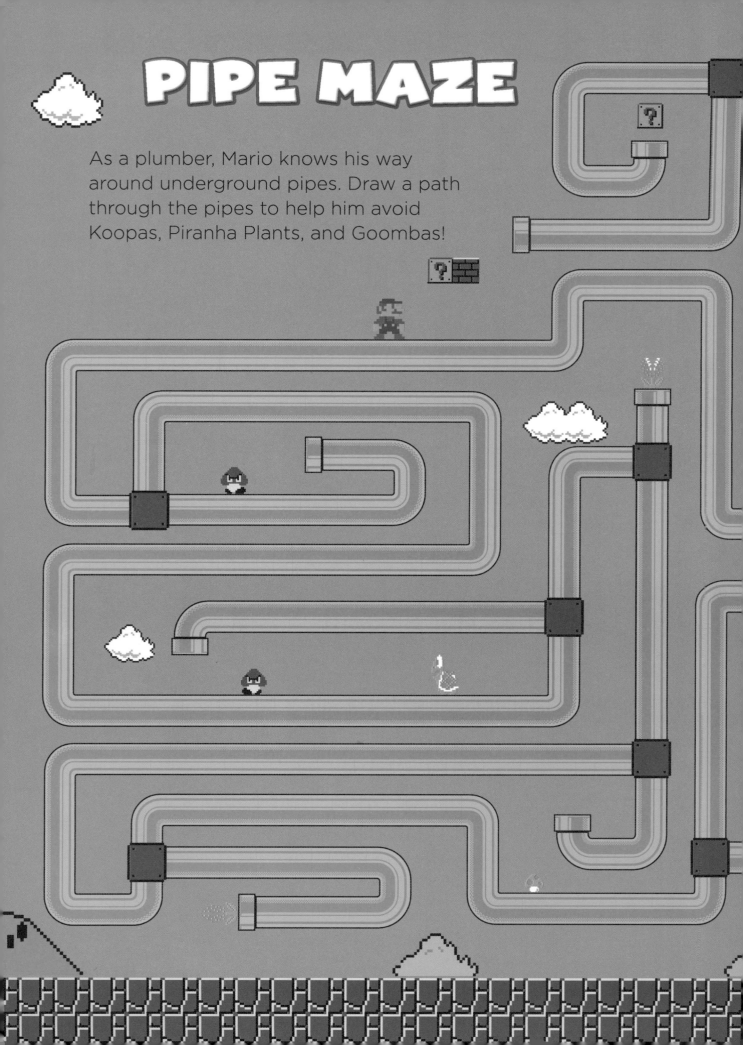

MARIO SCAVENGER HUNT

Many of the items in Super Mario Bros. games can also be found in real life. Look at the scavenger hunt list and see if you can find the items by the end of the day.

- [ ] star
- [ ] mushroom
- [ ] pipe
- [ ] coin
- [ ] block
- [ ] feather
- [ ] flower
- [ ] egg
- [ ] leaf

Princess Peach invited Mario to the castle to watch the shooting stars, but before he could get there, Bowser kidnapped the princess! Mario enlisted the help of the Lumas, friendly star creatures, to launch him into space in a special ship to search for the princess.

To find out the name of the ship, start at the arrow, and, going clockwise around the circle, write every third letter in order on the blanks.

_ _ _ _ _ _ _ _ _   _ _ _ _ _

CAST OF CHARACTERS

Which Super Mario Bros. character are you most like?
Circle your answers to the questions below.
Then check the answer key to find your match.

What is your favorite color?

- **A.** Pink
- **B.** Green
- **C.** Red
- **D.** Yellow

If you had to wear the same outfit every day, which would you pick?

- **A.** Something fancy
- **B.** Something comfortable
- **C.** Something casual
- **D.** Something intimidating

Of the following, which would you most like to do?

- **A.** Rule a kingdom
- **B.** Help friends
- **C.** Save the day
- **D.** Wreak havoc

What word would family and friends most likely use to describe you?

- **A.** Royal
- **B.** Loyal
- **C.** Brave
- **D.** Cunning

Where would you most like to live?

- **A.** A spacious castle
- **B.** On an island
- **C.** Always on the go
- **D.** Wherever I want

Answer Key

If you answered with mostly
A's: You're like Princess Peach!
B's: You're like Yoshi!
C's: You're like Mario!
D's: You're like Bowser!

PLAY SUDOKU!

Mario often has to outsmart Bowser to save the day. Practice your problem-solving skills by completing the puzzle. Here's the catch: each column and row must contain only one instance of each character.

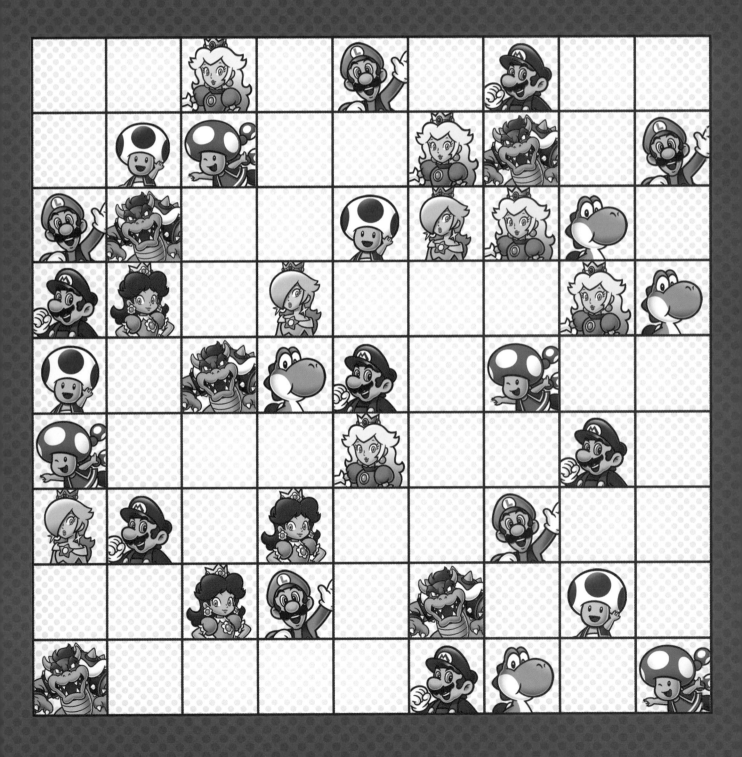

SHADOWY FIGURES

Can you identify Mario and his friends
and foes by their shadows below?

The music in the Super Mario Bros. series is just as popular and iconic as its characters. From the exciting **Overworld** theme to the foreboding **Castle** theme, the music sets the tone of the action.

Look at each of the scenes from the original **Super Mario Bros.** video game. Can you remember the music that goes along with each one?

OVERWORLD

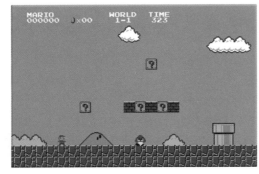

UNDERGROUND

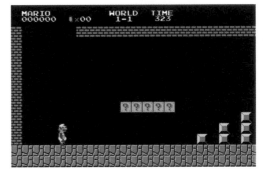

UNDERWATER

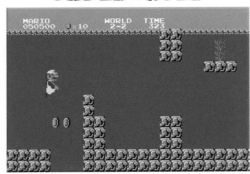

CASTLE

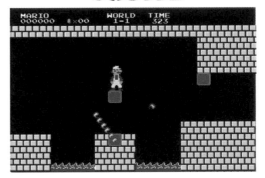

STARMAN

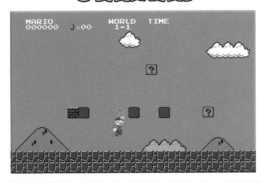

DID YOU KNOW?

The six main themes for Super Mario Bros. were created by Nintendo sound designer Koji Kondo.

FLIP BOOK

Mario and his friends are always on the move.
See them in action by making your own flip book!

Instructions
1. Cut out all the pages of the flip book.
2. Put the pages in order from 1 to 12.
3. Clip the pages together at the left with a binder clip.
4. Flip the pages quickly to see what Mario does next!

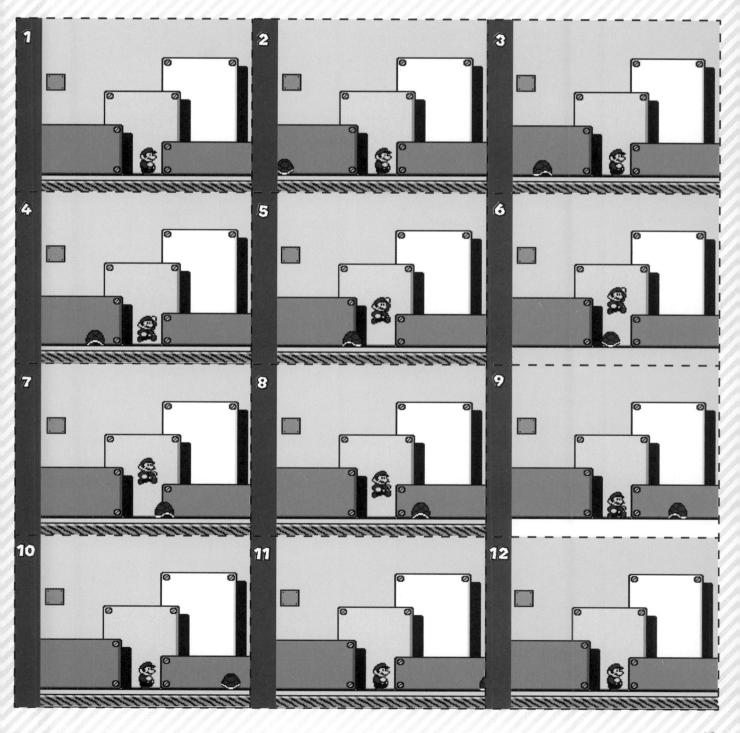

Bonus: If you turn the book upside down, you'll have another flip book!

FLIP BOOK

Instructions
1. Cut out all the pages of the flip book.
2. Put the pages in order from 1 to 12.
3. Clip the pages together at the left with a binder clip.
4. Flip the pages quickly to see what Yoshi does next!

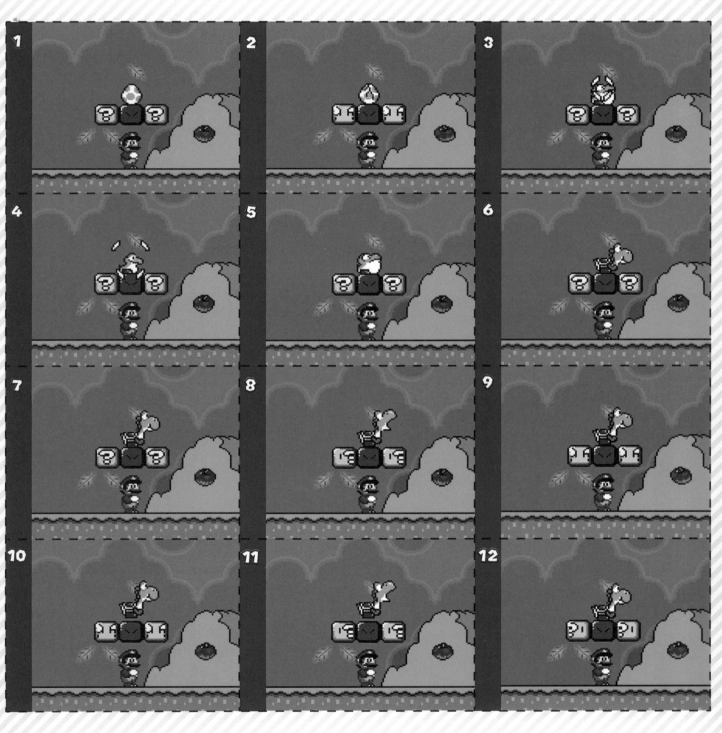

POWER UP!

Throughout his journey, Mario uses different
items to gain special powers.
How well do you remember the colors of each item?
Color the items below, then
check your answers on page 65.

Fire Flower

Super Mushroom

Super Star

1-UP Mushroom

If the cap fits . . .

There are also certain hats that Mario can wear to give him special abilities. Unscramble the words in bold to find out more!

1. The **TEMLA** cap turns Mario a shiny
   silver color.

   _____

2. The **NWGI** cap allows Mario to fly.

   _____

YOU BE THE CREATOR!

Have fun by using your favorite Mario catchphrases from page 35 to complete this comic strip. When you are done, color it.

SEEK AND FIND

Coins are the main currency in Mushroom Kingdom. On his way to save Princess Peach, Mario collects many of these shiny gold items. Can you help him collect **70** gold coins by circling them?

Power-Up Challenge: Can you find one item in your room that starts with each of the letters in the word COIN?

How many coins does Mario need to collect in order to get an extra life?
A. 50 **B.** 100 **C.** 200 **D.** 1,000

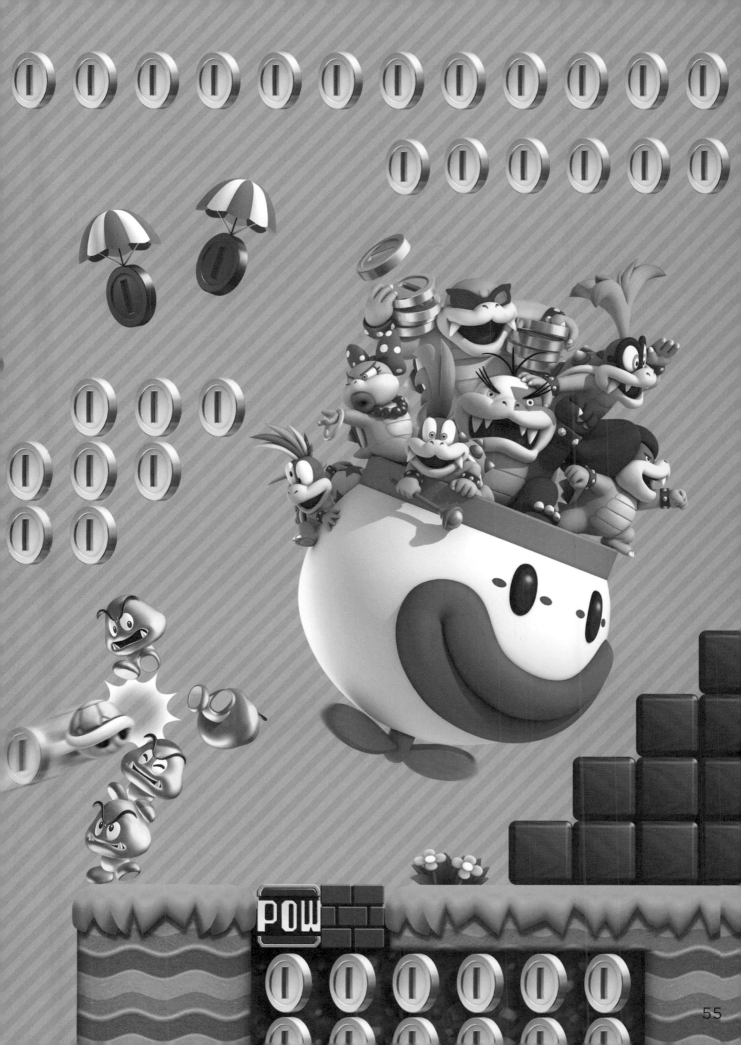

IN THE GAME

What would you be if you could create your own Super Mario character? **DRAW IT!**

What skills or abilities would you have?

_____

_____

_____

_____

How would you help Mario and Princess Peach save the day?

_____

_____

_____

_____

_____

PRINCESS PEACH'S CASTLE

Fun Facts

- Princess Peach's Castle is in Mushroom Kingdom.
- The castle is the home of Princess Peach, as well as Toad and many other royal attendants.
- The castle has a high tower and several large wings.
- One of the most prominent features of the castle is the large stained glass window bearing Princess Peach's likeness.

Using the key on the next page, color the stained glass window.

KEY

PINK = 1   YELLOW = 2   RED = 3   PURPLE = 4
GREEN = 5   MAGENTA = 6   ORANGE = 7   PEACH = 8
WHITE = 9   SKY BLUE = 10   BLUE = 11

59

Here we go!

In the **New Super Mario Bros. U** video game, Princess Peach is captured by Bowser and the Kooplings. With the help of different Yoshis, Mario and Luigi must travel across this new land and find a way to save Peach again. How many differences can you find?

GAME BREAK!

WELCOME TO MY CASTLE.

GAMING IN PROGRESS

PROCEED WITH CAUTION

ANSWERS

Page 16

B

Page 18–19

I	E	V	Q	L	E	M	M	Y	T	S	E	V	R
H	U	O	P	A	H	V	O	B	N	T	M	O	J
G	L	Y	E	R	S	E	R	C	T	V	G	Z	R
U	A	E	A	O	B	C	T	M	F	E	I	G	E
U	R	I	P	Y	E	Z	O	E	M	G	W	L	S
V	R	C	E	S	V	E	N	P	Y	L	D	O	W
T	Y	I	O	A	Q	W	D	S	G	R	U	C	O
C	O	W	E	N	D	Y	E	S	G	V	L	H	B
D	E	V	E	I	P	S	U	S	I	N	C	X	E

Page 27

Page 35

"Yippee!"
"Here we go!"
"Oh yeah, Mario time!"
"It's-a me, Mario!"
"Mamma Mia!"

Page 39

In the bottom picture, some of Morton's magic is missing, Lemmy's ball is missing, Iggy's wand is missing, Roy's glasses are now blue, and Bowser Jr.'s clown car is missing the red marks near the eyes.

Pages 40–41

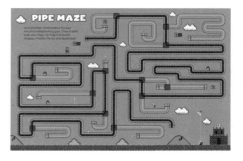

Page 43

Starship Mario

Page 46

Page 47

1. Princess Peach
2. Mario
3. Toad
4. Luigi
5. Yoshi
6. Toadette
7. Bowser
8. Bowser Jr.

Page 51

1. metal
2. wing

Page 54

B

Page 60

9. In the bottom picture, the rainbow is missing, Toad and Blue Yoshi are missing, the super acorn is now a super mushroom, Piranha Plant is missing, the flowers on the hill are missing, a Monty Mole is missing, the red Koopa is now a green Koopa, the yellow pipe is now a green pipe, and the winged Goomba is now a Goomba.